Shabba me whiskers! Andy Stanton's *Mr Gum* is winner of the Roald Dahl Funny Prize, the Red House Children's Book Award AND the Blue Peter Book Award for The Most Fun Story With Pictures. AND he's been shortlisted for LOADS of other prizes too! It's barking bonkers!

PRAISE FOR *Mr Gum*:

'Do not even think about buying another book – This is gut-spillingly funty.' Alex, aged 13

'It's hilarious, it's brilliant . . . Stanton's the Guv'nor, The Boss.' Danny Baker, BBC London Radio

'Funniest book I have ever and will ever read . . . When I read this to my mum she burst out laughing and nearly wet herself . . . When I had finished the book I wanted to read it all over again it was so good.' Bryony, aged 8

'Funny? You bet.' Guardian

'Andy Stanton accumulates silliness and jokes in an irresistible, laughter-inducing romp.' Sunday Times

'Raucous, revoltingly rambunctious and nose-snortingly funny.' Daily Mail

'David Tazzyman's illustrations match the irreverent sparks of word wizardry with slapdash delight.' Junior Education

'This is weird, wacky and one in a million.' Primary Times

For Leah Thaxton, Katie Bennett and
the amazing David Tazzyman

EGMONT
We bring stories to life

Mr Gum and the Secret Hideout
First published 2010 by Egmont UK Limited, 239 Kensington High Street London W8 6SA

Text copyright © 2010 Andy Stanton
Illustration copyright © 2010 David Tazzyman

The moral rights of the author and illustrator have been asserted

ISBN 978 1 4052 5327 7

5 7 9 10 8 6

www.egmont.co.uk/mrgum

A CIP catalogue record for this title is available from the British Library

Printed and bound in Great Britain by the CPI Group

Mr Gum

and the Secret Hideout

Andy Stanton

Illustrated by David Tazzyman

EGMONT

Contents

Some of the crazy old townsfolk from Lamonic Bibber

Mrs Lovely

Friday O'Leary

Billy William the Third

Old Granny

Mr Gum

Alan Taylor

Polly

Martin Launderette

Chapter 1

The Secret Hideout

Mr Gum was a fierce old blister with a face as angry as a thousand walnuts and a big red beard which smelt of menace and beer. He hated children, animals, fun, comics, pop music, birthday parties, books, Christmas, the seaside, computer games, people called 'Colin', Mondays, Tuesdays, Wednesdays, Thursdays, Fri– Actually, it would probably be quicker to tell you what he liked instead. What he liked was snoozing in bed all day, being a horror and secret hideouts. And the secret hideout he was in right now was the best secret hideout he'd ever seen.

'This secret hideout's flippin' brilliant!' shouted Mr Gum as he paced up and down in his hobnail boots. 'It's got everythin'! Rats! Cockroaches! Pipes what keep drippin' slime everywhere! An' it stinks! It's like what I always imagined Heaven would be! An' best of all, no one's ever gonna find us here!'

'Yeah,' agreed Mr Gum's dreadful accomplice, a scrawny butcher by the name of Billy William the Third. Billy was standing by a great iron furnace, shovelling old bits of meat on to the flames. And not just any old old bits of meat, but the stalest, grubbiest, most appalling specimens imaginable. Strings of ancient entrails, withered old horse legs, rubbery turkey necks . . .

On they all went, on to the flames. Billy was covered in soot and he was dripping with gobs of hot fat, but he hardly noticed. And why? I don't know, I'm not him. He just didn't.

'Faster!' commanded Mr Gum, hopping from one foot to the other like an unstoppable quail. 'Shovel them entrails, Billy me boy! Chuck it on, chuck it on! An' stoke it all up with coal or I'll bash ya!'

'Right you are, Gummy me old rattler!'

laughed Billy, chucking on a piece of coal that was twice the size of a piece of coal that was half the size of the piece of coal I'm talking about.

ROAR! bellowed the furnace. A great long lick of flame flicked out and singed off Billy's eyebrows, cruel as a scarlet donkey.

'Ha ha ha!' cackled Billy, who loved to see people getting hurt. 'Someone jus' got their eyebrows burned off!' Then he realised who that someone was, and he let out a bloodcurdling howl.

'OOW!' yelled Billy, hopping up and down in agony. 'How come I gotta do all the shovellin' 'round here anyway? How come you ain't doin' none?'

'Shut up!' roared Mr Gum, whacking Billy over the head with a silk handkerchief. He didn't have a silk handkerchief, so he used a cricket bat instead. 'We gotta keep gettin' that power up! We can't afford to rest for a moment. Now, you carry on shovellin'. I gotta rest for a moment.'

Mr Gum threw himself down on a filthy old sofa he'd found on a rubbish tip, all covered with stains and moss. The cushions were cold and soggy, and a big rusty spring poked uncomfortably into his back, but Mr Gum was such a lazer he didn't really care.

'I tell ya, I love this secret hideout,' yawned Mr Gum as he lay there staring up at the ceiling, his hands behind his head and his head behind whatever was in front of his head, probably just a bit of air or something. 'This is the life, eh, Billy?'

'Yeah, this is the life,' said Billy.

'Yeah, this is the life,' said another voice.

'Who the blimmin' flip said that?' shouted Mr Gum.

'It was I!' cried a man, jumping out from behind the sofa.

'I'm Surprising Ben! I pop up here, I pop up there! Surprise! Surprise! I'm everywhere!'

And off he ran, giggling like a packed lunch.

'Well, that was surprisin',' scowled Mr Gum.

'It certainly was,' said Billy, chewing a piece of coal to see if he could turn it into a diamond but actually just hurting his teeth. 'Anyway,' he continued, spitting it into the fire. 'Soon we'll have a blaze so powerful it'll be the most powerful in history! Even more powerful than itself, even though that's impossible!'

'Yeah,' grinned Mr Gum, rubbing his hands

with glee. Then he rubbed his hands with brie, which is sort of the same but a lot smellier. 'An' the more powerful that blaze gets, the closer we gets to winnin' once an' for all!'

'Ha ha ha!' said Billy William. 'It's funty!'

And the rats they scuttled and the pipes dripped slime and the vats they bubbled and Billy he shovelled in the secret hideout where the two men hid, cos they were low-down villains and that's what they did.

Chapter 2

The Department of Clouds and Yogurts

Later that day, a nine-year-old girl and an oldish fellow in a nice friendly hat were sitting in the town square watching something very peculiar. It was the clouds. Every now and then one

would just fall out of the sky – **FLOOOOOB!** - and land on the ground – **BUFFSH!**. See? Very peculiar indeed.

Now, the nine-year-old girl was Polly and the oldish fellow was Friday O'Leary. And if you're thinking, 'Who even cares about them, not me, I like stories with heroes in, not stories with some idiotic little girl and a bloke who's named after a day of the week,' then I'm afraid you've just made an astonishing fool of yourself. Because

Polly and Friday *were* heroes. They were two of the best heroes the town of Lamonic Bibber had ever seen. They were as brave as bees, as true as trees, as cheerful as cheese and as knowledgeable as knees. Not so clever now, are you?

FLOOOOOB! BUFFFSH!

Another cloud flopped out of the sky and landed on a hen, startling it so much that it accidentally laid an egg out of its mouth.

'Hmm,' said Polly. She had a worried expression on her face and Friday had a bit of strawberry yogurt on his. Friday loved yogurts.

'Frides,' said Polly at length. 'Do you know what I'm a-thinkin'?'

'Maybe,' said Friday hopefully. 'Are you thinking, "I ought to go and buy Friday an enormous yogurt, he deserves it?"'

'No,' replied Polly. 'I'm a-thinkin' there's somethin' well strange goin' on with them clouds up there. I never done seen 'em fallin' out the sky before. It can't be no good, that's what I says.'

'Yes,' said Friday thoughtfully. 'Well, that was interesting,' he continued. 'Now let's go and get some delicious yogurts and not think about it ever again.'

'But, Frides, if we jus' ignore them clouds who knows what might happen?' frowned Polly. 'Jus' imagine. Without no clouds, there won't be no rain. Without no rain, the grass won't grow.

Without no grass, the cows'll die. Without no cows there won't be no milk. An' without no milk –'

'There won't be any yogurts!' cried Friday in alarm as another cloud fell down with a soft furry bang somewhere in the distance. 'We've got to do something, Polly! We've got to! We've got to! We've simply GOT to!'

''Xactly,' said Polly. 'So I was thinkin', why don't we starts up an office an' do some 'vestigations?'

'THE TRUTH IS A LEMON MERINGUE!' yelled Friday, as he sometimes liked to do. 'I've always wanted to work in an office!'

It was true.
Friday O'Leary had
done all sorts of jobs in
his time. He had been
an inventor, a travelling
musician, a sailor,
another sailor, an American
footballer, a fashion model,
a Lego model, the King
of Sweden, the Queen
of Sweden, the first
man never to have walked on the moon,

a jet pilot, a detective, a mountaineer who explored mountains, a fountaineer who explored fountains, a ninja, a stunt-car racer, a film star, an earthworm-tamer, a famous French chef called Monsieur Canard, a TV presenter and a professional apple.

'But all those jobs were completely boring!' said Friday, jumping up so high he almost hit the sun with his face, narrowly missing it by only 149.599 million kilometres. 'What I've always wanted is to work in an office. That's the life for me!'

So Friday went home and got some planks and nails, and after a few hours of hammering and saying, 'Ouch, I just hit my thumb with a hammer,' there they were, sitting in their brand-new office in the town square. It was so cool. There was a big desk with some pens and a stapler on it. And there was a clock on the wall so you could see what time it was and a broken clock next to it so you could see what time it wasn't. And there were some chairs to spin around on and a photocopier so you could copy words and a photocopier so you could copy words and a photocopier so you could copy words and a photocopier so you could copy words and a photocopier so you could copy words and a photocopier so you could copy words and a photocopier so you could copy words and a photocopier so you could copy words –

'Stop playin' with that photocopier, Frides,' said Polly, 'an' help me think up a brilliant name for our new office. Then we can get started on our 'vestigations.'

'OK,' said Friday. 'How about *"THE DEPARTMENT OF CLOUDS AND YOGURTS"*?'

It was a brilliant name, apart from the yogurt bit. But Friday would not give in, so that's what they called it.

Polly went home and got some paint, and together she and Friday made a wonderful sign to hang above the office door:

THE DEPARTMENT OF
CLOUDS AND YOGURTS
Established: 15 minutes ago

After it was painted, Polly added some glitter and stickers of hearts and ponies around the words and Friday hung some broccoli from it 'for good luck'. It looked excellent. And if you looked at it twice, it looked twice as excellent. But if you looked at it three times, it still only looked twice as excellent, which just goes to show, things can get a bit boring if you look at them too much.

Then Friday went and bought suits and ties for them both. And then they sat at the desk with their hands folded in front of them, looking extremely serious.

'Now, Mr Friday,' said Polly. 'I done some 'vestigations in my head an' I reckons all the clouds are probbly bein' mucked up cos of bad pollutions in the air.'

'Exactly, Mr Polly,' said Friday, who was busy sharpening his tie in the electric pencil-sharpener.

'So we gots to work out where all them pollutions is comin' from,' said Polly. 'That's our first job.'

'Yes,' agreed Friday. 'That's our first job.'

'Yes,' said a voice in the corner. 'That's our first job.'

'Who said that?' said Polly.

'It was I!' cried a man, jumping out of the wastepaper basket. *I'm Surprising Ben! I pop up here, I pop up there! Surprise! Surprise! I'm everywhere!*

And away he ran, giggling like a tortoise.

'That was quite surprising,' said Friday. 'But now it's time to get to work. I have here a map of Lamonic Bibber,' he said, unrolling a huge map from his sock. 'Now, look carefully, Mr Polly. I drew this map myself, many years ago. See, there's my signature in the corner.'

DRAWN BY FRIDAY 'LEONARDO' O'LEARY, NOVEMBER 14TH 1973

'I don't want to sound boastful or anything,' said Friday modestly, 'but this is probably the most incredible map anyone's ever drawn in the history of all human existence. Look, every street, every house, every hill in Lamonic Bibber – it's all there.

'Now,' he continued. 'We will go looking for the pollution. We will investigate a little of the town each day. Then we will come back and colour in bits of the map to show we've investigated them.

And also because we like colouring things in.'

'Hurrah!' laughed Polly, clapping her hands.

FLOOOOOB!
BUFFFSH-SH-SH!!

A big wheezy cloud flopped out of the sky and landed right outside the office.

'There's no time to wastes, Mr Friday,' said Polly as the poor bit of weather was licked up by a stray baby. 'We better start doin' our 'vestigations.'

Chapter 3

The Badsters Yick it Up

BOING!
BOING!
BOING!

'That's it, Billy me old demonic melon!' laughed Mr Gum as he **BOING!**ed up and down on his grimsters old sofa. 'Chuck that meat on the heat!'

'Right you are!' cackled Billy, shovelling a pile of horse bladders on to the fire where they exploded in a dirty shower known as 'Butcher's Fireworks'. 'But why we doin' all this again, Mr Gum, me old Spanish woodworm?'

'Cos it's our flippin' masterplan, Billy me boy,' growled Mr Gum, **BOING!**ing higher than ever. 'The more we heat up them stale meats, the more poison gases goes up that massive chimney an' in the air. An' the more poison gases goes in the air, the hotter an' nastier it gets in Lamonic Bibber. It's called "Townal Warmin'".'

'Oh, yeah,' laughed Billy. '"Townal Warmin'".' Now I remember. An' once that stupid town gets hot enough, then –'

'SPLASH!' finished Mr Gum, grinning so nastily that a nearby mouse dissolved with fright. 'The weather goes crazy, Lamonic Bibber falls in the sea an' then we rule over it forever!'

'How we gonna rule over it if it's fallen in

the sea?' asked Billy through a mouthful of coal dust.

'Oh, yeah,' said Mr Gum. 'I never thought of that. Well, forget it. We'll just stick to destroyin' Lamonic Bibber by makin' it fall in the sea. That's evil enough for now. OI!' he shouted. 'Why ain't you shovellin' that meat? Get back to work, you lazy old trumpet!'

'But there ain't no more meat *to* shovel,' whined Billy. 'Them horse bladders was the last of it. We run out, see?"

'Well, take yer stupid cap off an' chuck it on the blaze!' yelled Mr Gum. So Billy took off his butcher's cap and threw it on the furnace, where it quickly burnt to a crisp.

'Now burn yer apron!' yelled Mr Gum. 'Now burn yer shirt! Now burn yer trousers! Now burn yer boots! Now burn yer socks! Now burn yer pant – nah, on second thoughts keep yer pants on, you disgustin' lettuce.'

'Well, that's it then,' said Billy as he stood there in his grubby grey boxer shorts. 'We burnt all the meat. We burnt me clothes. There's nothin' left to burn.'

'What we gonna do now?' scowled Mr Gum, stroking his beard into the shape of a gigantic red question mark.

'There's only one thing for it,' said Billy. 'We gotta go an' get more meat off that strange little bloke what helped us out last time.'

'It's true,' growled Mr Gum. 'But we gotta be crafty, Billy der Willy der Wills. We gotta be so crafty 'bout it that even we hardly know what we're up to ourselves. What's that thing called when it's all dark an' there's that stupid thing in the sky what's not the sun but the other one what's not so big?'

'Night time?' suggested Billy.

'Yeah, that's it,' grinned Mr Gum. 'That's the time to do our evils, Billy me boy – "Night time". When no one can see us, when no one can catch us an' when no one can stinkin' well stop us!'

Chapter 4

'Vestigations and Birdseed

Old Granny sat out on the high street, creaking back and forth in her ancient rocking chair from before the War.

**FLOOOB!
BUUFFFFSH!**

'Terrible days!' she cried, as a cloud plummeted from the sky and landed on her hat. The air was hot and sticky, and so thick that Old Granny's raspy lungs could hardly breathe it down. But in all her life she'd never missed a single day of sitting outside in her chair, 'And I'm not going to let a bit of weather stop me now!' said she.

SLUUUUUUUUUUURRRRRRP!

Old Granny took a thoughtful suck at a six-mile long drinking-straw that led directly to her secret sherry supply. And she shook her head so hard that you could hear the sherry swishing around inside her skull.

'Terrrible days! Terrible days!' she cried. 'Terrible days indeed!'

Old Granny's drunken words followed Polly and Friday as they walked along the high street, kicking up clouds of dust from the cracked, dried pavement.

'Right, Mr Friday,' said Polly, wiping a single bead of sweat from her brow and a whole necklace of sweat from her neck. 'We gots to find out who's doin' all them pollutions. It's time for THE DEPARTMENT OF CLOUDS AN' YOGURTS to gets to work!'

'Are you the one who's doing all the pollution?' they asked a little girl called Peter.

'No,' she said. 'I'm just playing with my doll.'

'Are you the one who's doing all the pollution?' they asked David Casserole, the town mayor.

'No,' he said. 'I'm just playing with *my* doll.'

'Are you the one who's doing all the pollution?' they asked William Shakespeare.

'Probably not,' he said. 'You see, I've been dead for about five hundred years. Now leave me alone, I'm trying to write *Hamlet II – Yorick's Revenge.*'

'FRUSTRATERS!' exclaimed Polly at the end of a long morning's work. 'We done millions of 'vestigations an' no one knows nothin', an' it's all boilin' hot an' itchy an' I had ENOUGHS!'

'Let's go back to the office,' suggested Friday.

But just then, they came upon a forlorn-looking fellow sitting in a silver birdcage at the side of the road. It was Crazy Barry Fungus.

'Tweet tweet?' he said hopefully. 'Tweet tweet?'

Now, Crazy Barry Fungus suffered from a rare medical condition called 'Stupidity'. Or in other words, he thought he was a chaffinch. Most people just passed him by as if he wasn't there. But Polly was far too kind-hearted for that.

'Here you goes, little birdy,' she said, fishing a handful of birdseed from her skirt pocket.

'Tweet tweet,' said Crazy Barry, licking it

gratefully from her palm. It was the kindest thing anyone had done for him in years.

'I don't expect he can help us,' said Friday. 'He's only a chaffinch. He knows nothing of the danger our town is in.'

But as Crazy Barry Fungus watched his visitors go, a gleam of light came into his eyes. 'Tweet tweet,' he said thoughtfully. 'Tweet tweet tweet tweet tweet.'

Back at the office, Polly and Friday coloured in all the places they'd visited on the map. It was quite fun. Polly did her bits in pink and Friday did his bits in 'bunch-paraka', which was a new colour he had invented that morning.

'Well, Mr Polly,' said Friday. 'We covered quite a lot of the town today – but there are still a few places left to investigate. Now, how about a nice cup of tea?'

So Polly put the kettle on, Polly put the kettle

on, Polly put the kettle on –

'Hey, are you playin' with the photocopier again, Mr Friday?' said Polly.

'Sorry,' said Friday. 'Hey, let's have a rubber-band fight!'

But just then, the office door flew open – and there stood Crazy Barry Fungus, flapping away in his birdcage, his face full of excitement and his mouth full of birdseed.

'Tweet!' he cried as he struggled through the

doorway. 'Tweet tweet!'

'I think he wants to tell us somethin'!' said Polly. 'Come in, Mr Crazy! Come in!'

Very carefully, Crazy Barry Fungus bent his head and began spitting out a message on the floor. A message written in birdseed.

'I'm sorry I have to spell out messages in birdseed,' he spelt, 'but I cannot talk as I am only a chaffinch. But you were kind to me earlier, and now I want to help you in return. For I see –'

Then he ran out of birdseed and had to lick it all up off the floor and start spitting it out again to carry on with his message.

'I see a lot of strange things on my travels,' wrote Barry Fungus, 'and lately I have seen something very peculiar. Something very –'

Then he ran out of birdseed and had to lick it all up again.

'This is really, really disgusting,' said Friday – but Polly hushed him.

'Something very peculiar indeed,' spat Barry Fungus. 'I have seen mysterious comings and goings down by the river. Yes, down by the river, when it's late and only us chaffinches are awake!'

'Comin's an' goin's down by the river?' said Polly. 'But what's that gots to do with them pollutions?'

Crazy Barry Fungus ran out of birdseed and licked it up again.

'I do not know,' he spat. 'Maybe something. Maybe nothing at all. Maybe I am just a silly old featherbrain who doesn't know what he's on about. But –'

Lick lick lick. Spit spit spit.

'I think you should go down to the river tonight and investigate. That is all. Good day to you both.'

And – GULP-IT-DOWN-CHAFFINCH-BOY-YOU-GOTTA-GULP-IT-DOWN! – he swallowed all the birdseed in a single almighty gulp.

'Thank you,' said Polly as the helpful creature hopped out of the office.

'You're welcome, don't mention it,' replied Crazy Barry Fungus in a deep booming voice. 'I mean – tweet tweet tweet, I can't talk. I'm only a chaffinch!'

And off he hopped in his silver cage, chirping all the way.

'What a lunatic,' marvelled Friday, who was

busy measuring the desk to see if it had secretly shrunk since they'd last seen it. Friday had a theory that desks were always trying to shrink, in order to fool people.

'Well, lunatic or not, he's the only one what done helped us so far,' said Polly. 'I says we go down to the river tonight to sees what's whats!'

Chapter 5

Down by the Riverside

Night time, and two mysterious figures were creeping through the darkness in their hobnail boots. Actually they weren't all that mysterious. They were Mr Gum and Billy, obviously. Although Billy had burned all his clothes back in Chapter Three, he was wearing a brand new uniform of butcher's apron, cap and trousers. And why? Because butchers are like lizards and can grow their skins back at any time.

'Feel how hot it's gettin', Billy, me old funnel?' said Mr Gum as they walked along.

'Yeah,' laughed Billy William. 'The air's as thick as muck. An' look,' he remarked, snatching up a gigantic fly with bright blue wings and about eight million legs and poison dripping from its jaws. 'Dirty tropical weirdies everywhere!'

'Yeah,' agreed Mr Gum, kicking a nearby tarantula in the face. 'An' it's all down to the miracles of poisonous gases an' pollution!'

Laughing softly, Mr Gum and Billy William crept through the night, and all around them strange insects and animals buzzed and flapped and hooted. But after quite a bit of creeping, Mr Gum realised something was wrong.

'Billy,' whispered Mr Gum. 'Here we are, creepin' along, an' all this time we forgot about the First Rule of Evil.'

'Oh, yeah,' said Billy, slapping himself on the forehead. 'What is it again, I forgot.'

Mr Gum regarded him with a frown. 'You really are an idiot, Billy. The First Rule of Evil is:

> *Whenever you are goin' creepin'*
> *through the darkness,*
> *Sing an evil song as you go by!*

'Oh, yeah,' laughed Billy. 'Now I remember.'

And with that, the two villains started up with their evil song, and though they sung it soft on the wind, all over town children suddenly started having nightmares, and all the milk turned bad, and a horse in a nearby field went mad and started frothing at the mouth, and then a moth flew by and the horse started frothing at the moth. For the song was indeed a terrible evil affair, and it went a little bit sort of something like this:

THE TEN RULES OF EVIL

CHORUS:

It's the Ten Rules of Evil
It's the Ten Rules of Evil
An' you jus' will not believe all
Of them tricks we like to play!

Rule One, whenever you are
goin' creepin' through the darkness
Sing an evil song as you go by!
Rule Two, if you see happy children
watchin' cartoons
Turn the channel over so they cry!

Rule Three, if you see insects,
pick 'em up in a bag
An' chuck 'em in people's food!
Rule Four, if there's a knock
at your front door
Open it an' shout out
somethin' rude!

CHORUS:

It's the Ten Rules of Evil
It's the Ten Rules of Evil
Oh, you jus' will not believe all
Of them tricks we like to play!

Rule Five, if there's a great big
circus comin' to town
Beat up all the clowns an' all their friends!
Rule Six, if you see somebody readin' a book
Rip the last page out so they
can't find out how it ends!

Rule Seven, if you ever meet
the Devil in the moonlight
Kick him in the tail an' run away!
Rule Eight, if he tries to come after you
Run away a little bit more!

CHORUS:

It's the Ten Rules of Evil
It's the Ten Rules of Evil
Oh, you jus' will not believe all
Of them tricks we like to play!

Rule Nine, if you should ever
get invited to a party
Puke on all the guests an' make a fuss!
An' as for Rule Ten, well, we ain't gonna tell ya
Cos we don't want you to end up
Quite as evil as us!

*(Two hour drum solo played on Billy's head
with a 'silk handkerchief')*

FIN

'What a brilliant song that was,' said Mr Gum.

'Yeah,' said Billy William. 'What a brilliant song that was.'

'Yeah,' said a voice in the darkness. 'What a brilliant song that was.'

'Who's there?' shouted Mr Gum, turning this way and that, his bashing fists at the ready.

'I'll – oh, it's you.'

'That's right! It is I!' said Surprising Ben, jumping out from a bush.

'I pop up here, I pop up there! Surprise! Surprise! I'm everywhere!'

And off he ran, giggling like a moonbeam.

'I'm gettin' sick of Surprisin' Ben,' growled Mr Gum. 'Anyway, who cares – here we are at last.'

Yes, folks, Mr Gum and Billy had come to the Lamonic River, which is like the rest of Lamonic Bibber, only wetter and with more crisp packets floating around on it.

Swisheroo. Swisheroo. Swisheroo.

((((((

The soft waters lapped against the riverbank. The insects buzzed overhead. Somewhere in the distance a dog barked. Or maybe the dog was actually much closer than that, and just barking quietly to pretend it was further away than it seemed. Dogs can be crafty like that.

'Whadda we do now?' whispered Billy as they stood there on the hot, steaming riverbank, toads and vagabonds dribbling on their boots.

'Now we give the signal,' grinned Mr Gum, and he looked so awful in the smog and the fog that even Billy felt afraid and fell back a step. Still grinning, Mr Gum removed his hat to reveal an enormous candle made of sheep fat stuck on his pointy head.

'Light me up, Billy me boy,' whispered Mr Gum, so Billy lit a match by just looking at a match and hoping it would somehow light. Then he lit the candle on Mr Gum's head and all at once it blazed up with a horrible green and orange glow, like a Halloween pumpkin who simply will not behave. The ghastly light spilled over the scene, cutting through the smog and making Billy see all sorts of shapes and phantoms in the mist.

'Ha ha,' said the shapes and phantoms in the mist. 'We are shapes and phantoms in the mist.'

And then there was a whisper from downriver – 'That's it, lads! There's the signal!'

And something came gliding through the murky waters to meet them.

Chapter 6

The Midnight Meating

*S*wisheroo. *Swisheroo. Swisheroo.*

The waters lapped gently in the hot tropical night.

Chug. Chug.

The dark shape came slowly down the river.

Bzzzz. Bzzzzzzzz.

Swarms of mosquitoes, drawn to the candlelight, circled lazily around Mr Gum's head.

Phwick! Snark! Slurrrrp!

Billy flicked out his tongue and scoffed one down.

And lying hidden beneath a pebble, watching the whole horrid scene unfold, were Polly and Friday. Their eyes widened as the candle spat out the last of its grisly light.

'So Crazy Barry Fungus was right,' whispered Polly. 'There's well mysterious goin's on goin' on! An' it looks like Mr Gum's behind it all!'

Chug chug chug.

Slowly the thing on the river came into sight. It was an old-fashioned steamboat, its battered, patched-up sides lurching drunkenly in the moonlight. A paddlewheel on the side turned as it chugged along, and a huge funnel bloated out clouds of greyish-black smoke into the night sky. A ragged flag hung from the prow, showing a pig's skull with two pork chops crossed beneath.

'Shudder!' whispered Friday. 'They're flying the "Jolly Rasher"! They're I.M.P.s!'

'Imps?' said Polly. 'Like them little spiky things what runs round kitchens ruinin' the pancakes?'

'No, not imps,' said Friday. *'I.M.P.s! International Meat Pirates!'*

And then, all of a sudden a voice boomed out, a voice that chilled the blood in Polly's veins and froze the marrow in her vegetable patch.

'Fifty degrees starboard! Pump

the pedals! Throw the ropes! Stoke the engine! Starbuck – make me a cup of coffee, semi-skimmed milk, two sugars! Look lively, lads! All hands on deck!'

And now Polly could see him, a puffed-up little dandelion of a fellow standing at the helm, his grey hair teetering on his head and his right arm thrust forward, pointing the way. He looked a lot scruffier than when she'd last met him, and his nose hadn't been polished for quite some time. But there could be no mistaking who it was.

'It's George Washington!' trembled Polly. 'I mean – it's Captain Brazil!'

And Polly was right to tremble, because Captain Brazil was an absolute CRAZER. He was the terror of the high seas and his adventures were legendary. For instance, he had once killed a sailor just by looking at him for ten minutes. And then shooting him through the heart with a pistol. And you know the Lost City of Atlantis that lies beneath the ocean waves? Well, it was Captain

Brazil who had lost it. It had fallen out of his pocket when he was playing marbles. Once he had commanded the *Nantucket Tickler*, a fine sailing ship indeed, but lately he had fallen upon hard times and was reduced to this, a grotty little steamer called the *Sirloin* which stank of sweat and rum.

'What on earth's he doin' here?' whispered Polly. 'He's as mad as a bulldozer's cousin!'

STOP THE BOAT!

'Stop the boat!' commanded Captain Brazil, so loudly that his hair automatically stuffed itself into his ears to stop him from going deaf.

'Aye aye, sir!' said Starbuck, the Second Mate.

'Now quickly start the boat again and then stop it so everyone falls over!' commanded Captain Brazil.

'Aye aye, sir!' said Starbuck, quickly starting the boat and then stopping it so everyone fell over.

'Now say, "That was completely pointless!"' commanded Captain Brazil.

'That was completely pointless!' said the crew.

'Good work, men. Right. Lower the gangway – and look lively about it!'

'Aye aye, sir,' laughed one of the sailors, an enormous hulking nit by the name of Brendan Jawsnapper. His muscular arms bulged as he turned the handle, and down creaked the gangway on to the riverbank.

'Make way, make way!' cried Captain Brazil, disappearing from sight. 'I am coming ashore!'

For a couple of minutes nothing happened. The *Sirloin* sat bobbing gently in the water, its engine purring quietly and its funnel miaowing loudly.

'What's takin' him so long?' snarled Mr Gum. A couple more minutes passed. Then a couple more. Then there was a long flushing sound and finally Captain Brazil stepped ashore, wiping his hands on Nimpy Windowmash, the First Mate.

'Sorry about that, I was doing a poo,' said Captain Brazil with a graceful bow. 'Now, Mr Gum. What brings you back so soon?'

But then he spotted Billy William and a look of astonished wonder came over his weather-beaten face.

'Elizabeth!' cried Captain Brazil, throwing his arms wildly about the startled butcher.

'My dear Elizabeth! What mean you, turning up like this after all these years? You broke my heart once – must you come back now to break it all over again?'

And kissing Billy passionately on the lips, the little captain threw himself down into the long grass and began weeping uncontrollably.

'Why must love be so painful?' he protested. 'Why, Elizabeth, why? Why, Elizabeth, why? Why, Elizabeth, w–'

'Um, 'scuse me, you complete weirdo,' said Mr Gum, after about half an hour of this. 'But that ain't no beautiful lady, it's jus' Billy.'

'So it is,' said Captain Brazil, standing up and brushing himself off. 'Sorry about that. Now, gentlemen. What can I do for you on this fine night? Surely ye haven't run out of meat already?'

'Well, we have,' snarled Mr Gum. 'So give us some more – or I'll wallop you up!'

'Yeah,' grinned Billy. 'An' the rottener

the better!'

'So be it,' said Captain Brazil grandly. 'Men – unleash the cargo!'

'Aye aye, sir,' said Brendan Jawsnapper. There was a mighty snap as he bit through a rope, and then

BUMP!
JOSTLE!
BASH!

A great heap of barrels came rolling down the

gangway like an avalanche made of wood. One hundred barrels! Two hundred barrels! Three hundred barrels! Yes, if you like barrels, this is definitely the scene for you!

Mr Gum opened the first barrel by telling Billy to open the first barrel. Then the two villains hunched eagerly over it, their eyes agleam in the moonlight.

'Meat,' drawled Mr Gum, reaching in and scooping up a sloppy green and red mess as if it were a heap of fine emeralds and rubies.

'Rotted to perfection!' said Billy, taking a long admiring sniff.

'I don't understand,' said Captain Brazil. 'We have many fine meats aboard my vessel. But each time you come, you take only the poorest and dirtiest meats. Why, gentlemen, why?'

'Cos they burn the best,' said Billy proudly. 'An' they make the most poisonous-est gases what mucks up the weather. See, me an' Mr Gum here is hidin' out in a secret hideout –'

'Shut up, you muncher!' hissed Mr Gum, boxing Billy's ears with a cardboard box. 'You never know who might be listenin'!'

'Well, I always knows who might be listenin'!' announced Polly as she and Friday sprang up from under their pebble. 'THE DEPARTMENT OF CLOUDS AN' YOGURTS, that's who! Freeze, you naughties – you're all under arrests!'

Chapter 7

Prisoners!

'Who be these two whippersnaps?' roared Captain Brazil as Friday and Polly emerged from the darkness.

'I'll tell you who they be,' snarled Mr Gum so furiously that the *Official Mr Gum Fury-O-Meter* strapped to his chin went all the way up to 1000 and then exploded in a spray of glass and mercury. 'They be MEDDLERS! Always gettin' in the way of me business!'

'Well, you hasn't gots no business doin' that sorts of business,' said Polly. 'It's a nasty business, an' it's our business to stop it. You're all under arrests for so many reasons I can't even be bothered to count them all, you flibs!'

'Exactly,' said Friday, taking out his notebook. 'Now, tell us your names so we can send you to the prisons where you truly belong.'

'Me name's Little Carlos,' pleaded Mr Gum, dropping to his knees and clutching pitifully at Friday's ankle. 'I am only a poor shepherd boy from Portugal and I ain't got no idea what's goin' on. Please don't arrest me – for then who will look after me faithful sheep, Splinters?'

'That's me,' said Billy William the Third, dropping to all fours and nibbling at Friday's other ankle. 'Baaa! I'm Splinters the sheep. Baaaa!

Baaaaa! Hello.'

'Oh, dear,' said Friday in confusion. 'I think we've arrested the wrong people, Mr Polly.'

'Frides, they're not no innocent shepherds an' sheep, they're lyin'!' said Polly. But in all the confusion, no one noticed that big beefy whaler of a sailor, Brendan Jawsnapper. He had one more barrel left, the biggest of the lot. And now he was creeping along the deck of the *Sirloin*. His tattooed muscles rippled as he hoisted that barrel over his head . . . And then . . .

SPLARSHINGTON!

A slew of pig intestines, horse livers and albatross hearts rained down on the heroes.

'URGH!' said Polly.

'URGH!' said Friday.

Everyone waited, in case Surprising Ben was about to pop up and say 'URGH!' as well.

But he didn't. You see, that was actually the most surprising thing about Surprising Ben – just when you expected him to surprise you he surprised you by not surprising you at all.

'Yaar-har-har!' laughed Captain Brazil, who had recently been listening to a CD called **Teach Yourself to Laugh Like a Pirate in Ten Easy Lessons**. 'Get 'em, mateys! We'll take 'em prisoner an' steam off to China an' sell 'em to the circus, yaar-har-har!'

'Oh, no!' said Friday, as the crew of the *Sirloin* came smashing down the gangway to get them. 'Whatever's going to become of us?'

'He jus' said,' replied Polly, as she was hoisted off her feet. 'He's gonna take us prisoner an' steam off to China an' sell us to the circus.'

'Oh, right,' said Friday, who was dangling over Starbuck's shoulder. 'I couldn't hear. I had some sheep's lungs in my ear.'

'HA HA! So much for the DEPARTMENT OF CLOUDS AN' YOGURTS!' laughed Mr Gum, as he watched the heroes being bundled aboard. 'Looks like we're free to do our evils after all!'

'Yeah!' said Billy William the Third.

And the last thing Polly saw as the boat pulled away was Mr Gum and Billy tap-dancing on the barrels of meat, singing 'The Ten Rules of Evil' and slapping their thighs with bits of bone and gristle.

Captain Brazil stood on deck, looking down with contempt on the prisoners as they struggled in the sailors' brawny arms. Then he realised he wasn't tall enough to look down with contempt on the prisoners as they struggled in the sailors' brawny arms, so he stood on a little stool and looked down with contempt on the prisoners as they struggled in the sailors' brawny arms.

'Throw 'em in the brig!' he exclaimed.

'NO!' protested Friday. 'Not the brig! Anything but the brig! Please, I beg you – not the brig! If you've an ounce of mercy in you, please – do not throw us in the brig! Also, what is a "brig", by the way?'

'It be the ship's prison, where the rats'll pick at yer toenails to get at the tasty cheese, an' the weevils'll make their homes in yer nostrils,' said Captain Brazil.

And even as he spoke, Brendan Jawsnapper threw open a heavy iron door and tossed the heroes inside as easily as if they were a couple of bags of flour.

KLANK! went the door.

CLICK! went the lock.

'OH, THE CAMPTOWN LADIES SING THIS SONG, DOO DAH!

DOO   DAH!' went the ringtone on Captain Brazil's mobile phone.

And they were prisoners!

Chapter 8

Ship's Biscuit

And now began an ordeal so awful that Friday and Polly would remember it for the rest of their lives, apart from Friday, who instantly forgot it as soon as it was over. For hour upon hour the two friends sat in the cold damp gloom of the brig, with only a thin crack of light coming

from under the door by which to see.

From time to time a small metal hatch would open and a sailor would throw in some food. It was always but a single crumb of bread, except for one time when the hatch opened and in came eight roast chickens, gravy, garden peas, buttered parsnips, a choice of side salad or spicy Cajun potato wedges and a 'Smiley Meal' plastic toy.

'Oops,' said the sailor from the other side of the hatch. 'I accidentally threw the prisoners our supper instead.'

But apart from this stroke of good fortune, it was a miserable time. The two friends hardly talked, but sat in silence, Polly wondering what was to become of her beloved hometown of Lamonic Bibber, and Friday thinking of new flavours for yogurts. Slowly, slowly the night passed as the *Sirloin* chugged its way upriver, heading for the open sea and then China. The engine thrummed and the big wheel on the side of the boat turned and splashed, turned and splashed, turned and splashed again.

Captain Brazil's cabin must have been directly above the brig, for sometimes Polly could hear him stamping around and moaning, 'Oh, Elizabeth! Elizabeth! Come back to me, Elizabeth!' And then it seemed she could hear him weeping, and soon after – 'More rum! Starbuck! Bring me more rum!' Then all would be silent for a while until the stamping began once more, and the moaning. 'Oh, Elizabeth! Elizabeth! How I love thee, sweet Elizabeth!'

And so the long night passed, in wails and moans and splashes and groans and sighs. Did Polly fall asleep? She did not know, for in that near-darkness, what was real and what was not became blurred and mixed together, like when you're on a 'plane with your mum and dad and you pour all the pepper and salt and little pots of milk and things into your orange juice in that plastic cup they give you and you even put in that little face-wipe that smells of lemons, and then you stir it around and it looks like puke and then you dare your sister to drink it and then your mum says, 'Stop that, act your age!' and then the stewardess comes round to collect everyone's stuff and your mum hands her your disgusting cup and says, 'Sorry about my children, they're very immature.'

Yes, in that near-darkness, what was real and what was not became blurred and mixed together.

So did Polly fall asleep? She thought she did. For surely it must have been a dream, the way she felt. As if every part of her body was as light as a cloud, as light as a fluffy little cloud . . . And then suddenly, standing before her, she seemed to see a boy whose honest face she knew well.

'Hello, child,' said the boy, though he was no older than she. 'I like your suit and tie. But tell me – what are they feeding you in this place?'

'Mostly jus' some crumbs,' exclaimed Polly glumly.

'I see,' said the lad. 'And do they not feed you Ship's Biscuit?'

'No,' said Polly. 'We never gets no Ship's Biscuit.'

'Well,' laughed the boy kindly. 'Perhaps you don't need any. Perhaps you already have all the biscuit you need.'

And then the moment was gone – if it had ever really happened. But as Polly sat shivering and blinking in the gloom, she replayed the strange dream over and over in her mind.

'"Perhaps you already gots all the biscuit what you need,"' she murmured. 'What did that 'mazin' spirit mean?' For she felt sure she had just been visited by the Spirit of the Rainbow, who was a force for good and could do mysterious things like get into your dreams and give you clues.

'But I hasn't got no biscuits,' she said. 'Unless . . .'

Polly patted the jacket of her suit – and there was a small lump in the top pocket!

'Could it be?' she wondered . . . She reached into the pocket and her hand closed on something rough and crunchy. It was Alan Taylor, her tiny gingerbread friend!

'So you're the "ship's biscuit"!' marvelled Polly. Alan Taylor was fast asleep and there was a sign around his neck which said '*HIBERNATING*

– *DO NOT DISTURB UNTIL SPRING*'. He looked ever so peaceful and his electric muscles whirred gently in time with his delightful sugary snores.

'Sorry, A. T., but we needs you now,' whispered Polly, tickling him softly under the chin with a weevil.

'Zzzz,' snored Alan Taylor. 'Zzz – hee hee! Ooh, that tickles! Zzzz – hee hee!'

And then he was awake and standing in the palm of her hand, his electric muscles glowing feebly in the gloom.

'Polly!' he blinked. 'Is it spring yet?'

'No,' whispered Polly, 'but I'm ever so glads to see you, cos me an' Frides is in the biggest trouble of our lives.'

And then Friday awoke and the three friends hugged each other in the darkness and Friday asked Alan Taylor what he was doing in Polly's pocket in the first place.

'Simple,' replied Alan Taylor. 'Every year, we

gingerbread men like to find a nice warm pocket in which to curl up and hibernate. It is the way of my people. Always has been and always will be.'

'Well, I'm jus' glad you picked my pocket to sleep in, you glorious little nibbly,' said Polly. 'By the way, do you thinks you can get out that little crack under the door?'

'For enormous overweight giants like you two it would be impossible,' said Alan Taylor proudly. 'But my tiny size means I can pass through even the smallest cracks! It is the way of my people.'

And he slid under the door like a thing sliding under another thing and he was gone.

A few minutes later they heard a scrabbling noise outside the door and then the sound of a key turning in the lock.

'Can you open the door?' Alan Taylor whispered. 'It's too heavy for me.'

'Oh, so now you want the help of us "enormous overweight giants", do you?' said

Friday. But Polly pushed the door open and the exhausted biscuit tumbled back in, clutching a big brass key almost as large as himself.

'The key was hanging around the First Mate's neck,' he explained. 'I managed to hop up on to his fat stomach and remove it without waking him. It is the way of my people.'

'Well, what are we waiting for?' said Friday. 'THE TRUTH IS A LEMON MERINGUE! Let's get out of here!'

'I don't think that would be a good idea,' said Alan Taylor. 'We could make it up to the deck but there's nowhere to run. And we can't jump overboard, because I noticed the sea was full of massive sharks and krakens and that guy out of *Pirates of the Caribbean* who's got tentacles all over his face.'

'Hmm,' said Polly, who was examining some ropes and old sacks in one corner of the brig.

'Elizabeth, oh, my sweet Elizabeth!' moaned Captain Brazil from his cabin.

'Hmm,' said Polly again. 'Listen up, gang, not with jus' one or two of your ears but with ev'ry single last one of 'em. Cos I think I gots a 'genious plan.'

Chapter 9

The Captain and Elizabeth

'Twas the wee hours of the morn and the *Sirloin* chugged slowly through the mist and the fog. 'Twas the wee hours of the morn when things get strange and ghostly, and Captain Brazil could not sleep. 'Twas the wee hours of the morn and he was stumbling around his cramped wooden cabin, a-frighted by the spectres of the past.

'*Remember meeeeeee?*' he seemed to hear a papery voice whisper. '*I am the ghost of that cabin boy who you dressed up as a cake and threw to the sharks.*'

'Leave me alone!' sobbed Captain Brazil, tearing a chart from the wall and shredding it to bits.

'*Remember meeeee?*' said another voice. '*I am the ghost of Captain Barnaby Weed! You sank my ship just because I didn't invite you to my party! But now I'll sink YOU!*'

'Get out of my head, you horrors!' begged Captain Brazil. He picked up a decanter of rum and hurled it at the wall. 'Leave me aloooooone!'

But of all the faces from the past, one was even more painful than the rest. 'Oh, Elizabeth,

Elizabeth!' cried Captain Brazil in anguish and also in English. Why did you leave me, Elizabeth? Oh, what I would give to hear you knock-knock-knocking at my cabin door this moment! Oh, how I would –'

KNOCK KNOCK KNOCK!

'What?!' cried the captain, turning on his heel, his tailcoat flying out behind him. His drunken eyes rolled madly in his head. 'Who goes there? Who dare troubles me at such an hour? Yargh!'

Squinting through the smoked glass he could just make out a tall figure, a figure with long flowing hair . . .

'Is it possible?' whispered Captain Brazil. Trembling like an oyster-butler, he staggered to the door and threw it wide open to the cold grey of the early sea dawn and the figure standing before him.

'Hello,' said the figure in a high-pitched voice. 'You know that beautiful woman you're

always going on about? What's her name again,
I've forgotten?'

'Tis E-Elizabeth,' stammered Captain Brazil.

'Oh, yeah,' replied the strange visitor. 'Well,
that's me. I'm Elizabeth.'

And with that, Elizabeth stepped into
the light. Her hair was long and ropey, her
dress looked a bit like an old sack with flowers
drawn on in biro, and her lipstick looked like it
might have been done with an orange crayon.
But Captain Brazil would have recognised her

anywhere, especially as he was unbelievably drunk on rum.

'By the shilly-shally fish of the Sea of Procrastination!' he cried. ''Tis you, 'tis really you! Oh, Elizabeth! I ought to shower you in kisses and spicy fruits! But tell me – why did you leave me, all those years ago? Why did you turn your back on me and walk out of my life like an unfeeling potato?'

'Um . . . I had to sew a button on to my dress,'

replied Elizabeth.

'What, you've been sewing on a button for the last forty years?' said Captain Brazil in astonishment.

'It was a very big button,' replied Elizabeth solemnly. 'But now I have returned to be by your side.'

'Oh, Elizabeth,' said Captain Brazil, dropping to his knee and accidentally squishing a weevil. 'Won't you say those sweet words you used to say to me? Those sweet words of love that always took the trouble from my brow and made me feel like a happy little baby in a bucket of seahorses?'

'Um . . . OK,' said Elizabeth. 'What were they again?'

'Fie! Fie! Fie!' cried Captain Brazil. He leapt to his feet and drew his cutlass. 'Can thou not remember those sweet words? Perhaps thou art not Elizabeth after all!'

'THE TRUTH IS A LEMON MERINGUE!' cried

Elizabeth in fright. 'No, I'm definitely Elizabeth, I'm sure of it!'

'Stop stalling for time and say those words!' bellowed Captain Brazil, pressing the tip of the cutlass against Elizabeth's neck.

'OK,' gasped Elizabeth. And screwing her eyes shut in concentration, she bent down and whispered into the captain's ear.

'Captain Brazil,' she whispered,

'From the sun-coasts of Jamaica
to the icy shores of Sweden
From the tip of Argentina
to the springs of Manderley
I will always love you, Captain,
for you guide me through the oceans
La la la la
La la la la
La la la la
Something else.'

'These are not the words you used to say!' cried Captain Brazil. 'You used to say, "Hey, Captain Brazil, buy me a pair of new shoes or I'll knock your block off." But I like these new words even better,' he said, wiping a tear from his cheek. 'They are beautiful. Now, you have proved you are probably Elizabeth after all and I will do anything for you.'

'Hmm,' said Elizabeth, flinging herself into Captain Brazil's lap and tenderly stroking his earlobe. 'Actually, there is something I would like you to do, my love.'

'Anything for you, my darling,' breathed Captain Brazil, gently caressing Elizabeth's shoe. 'Anything at all.'

'Well, then,' said Elizabeth. 'I would like you to turn this steamship around and head back to Lamonic Bibber right now. And then I'd like you to release the prisoners and bid them farewell. Oh, and you know Friday O'Leary?' she added.

'You should definitely give him some yogurts. He likes yogurts.'

'It is done, m'lady, it is done!' cried Captain Brazil. 'CREW!' he thundered, and at once his men came running. 'TURN AROUND! EIGHT MILLION DEGREES STARBOARD! CHECK THE RUDDER! FLY THE FLAG! MAN THE THINGS! DO THE STUFF!'

'Thank you, my darling,' said Elizabeth. 'Now, I must away and prepare for our wedding in the morning.'

'Oh, Elizabeth,' cried Captain Brazil as the *Sirloin* started to turn. 'You have made me the happiest man alive. Come on, crew! Shake a leg! We're heading back to Lamonic Bibber! And I'm getting married in the mo-oor-ning!'

Chapter 10

Old Granny on the Hoof

The sun was rising when they reached Lamonic Bibber, but it was not a nice sun. It was fierce and red and bloody and it gazed down like a terrifying football that had gone insane with its own power to score goals. The yellow clouds swarmed sulkily overhead. Strangely-coloured worms and mosquitoes roamed freely in the sweltering heat. A seagull tried desperately to open a bottle of suntan oil with its beak. It was a tropical paradise. OF DOOM.

'By the second-hand tutu of old Captain Ballerina!' exclaimed Captain Brazil as the *Sirloin* swayed drunkenly towards shore. 'The river has burst its banks and 'tis flooding the land! Yaar, yaar, yaar! It be terrible! Heave ho, mateys! We are here – though were it not for Elizabeth, I would never have returned to this accursed place! Nimpy! Release the prisoners!'

'Aye aye, cap'n,' said the First Mate, Nimpy Windowmash. He unlocked the brig and Polly and Friday stumbled out, coughing and gasping in the thick, crowded air.

'Prisoners,' announced Captain Brazil grandly. 'You are free to go. Now, be off with you and trouble me no more. Oh, I just remembered,' he added, turning towards Friday. 'Elizabeth asked me to give you these.' And he pressed a few pots of yogurt into Friday's hand.

'Excellent!' exclaimed Friday, putting them into his secret Yogurt-Storing Compartment, otherwise known as his mouth. 'I love yogurts.'

'An' so 'tis farewell,' said Captain Brazil, standing to attention and saluting until Polly and Friday were out of sight. 'And now to marry Elizabeth!'

But sadly for Captain Brazil, Elizabeth never

did show up that morning or even the next. And eventually he gave up waiting and headed back to sea.

'For the sea she never does let ye down,' he told his crew. 'An' there's adventures out there for the takin', me boys! With a heave an' a ho an' a bucket of wine, there's adventures out there for the takin'!'

'Come on!' cried Polly as she and Friday raced into town. 'There's no time to lose! We gots to get THE DEPARTMENT OF CLOUDS AN' YOGURTS rollin' again. We gots to 'vestigate every last buildin' and find them villainers!'

Overhead, the ugly clouds roiled and broiled and groiled. The rising waters snaked along after them and with every step, the air grew thicker and sludgier with the stench of rotten meat.

'Oh, no!' exclaimed Alan Taylor from Polly's pocket. 'I can't breathe this, I'm a vegetarian!'

Soon they were on the high street – but Polly barely recognised it. There was hardly anyone around, just a few people sitting quietly in shop doorways or stretched out hopelessly on the cracked and dusty ground.

'It's – so hot,' croaked the little girl called Peter. 'We can't – breathe!'

'And there's a – beached whale by the town hall!' gasped Martin Launderette, who ran the launderette.

'I'm not – a – beached whale!' replied Jonathan Ripples, the fattest man in town.

'Yes – you are,' croaked Martin Launderette unkindly.

FLOOOOB! BUFFFFFFFSSSH!

Clouds fell from the sky.

The sun beat down mercilessly.

Cactuses had started to grow through the pavements.

'Terrible days!' cawed flocks of brightly coloured parrots from the rooftops. 'Terrible days! Terrible days! Awk!'

Old Granny sat out in the middle of the street, rocking back and forth in her chair. 'Terrible days! Terrible days!' she muttered, taking a suck on her six-mile long straw. 'Temperatures rising! Rivers bursting their banks! A cactus growing under my feet! The world's turned upside-down!'

But THE *DEPARTMENT OF CLOUDS AND YOGURTS* had no time to spend listening to Old Granny's ramblings.

'Billy said they was hidin' out in a secret hideout,' said Polly. 'We gots to search everywhere we can think of an' even some places we can't!'

'We must leave no stone unturned!' said Friday, turning over a stone in case the secret hideout was underneath. 'Let's go!'

So Polly and Friday got the map from their office and all that morning they searched beneath the sweltering sun, colouring in bits of the map as they went.

And all that morning Old Granny rocked back and forth in her chair and shook her head. And all that morning the cactus grew higher and higher between her legs until she and her chair were ten feet off the ground. The heat was almost unbearable but Old Granny was a tough old macaroon and she would not be moved, not even when the first muddy waters from the river began flooding the high street.

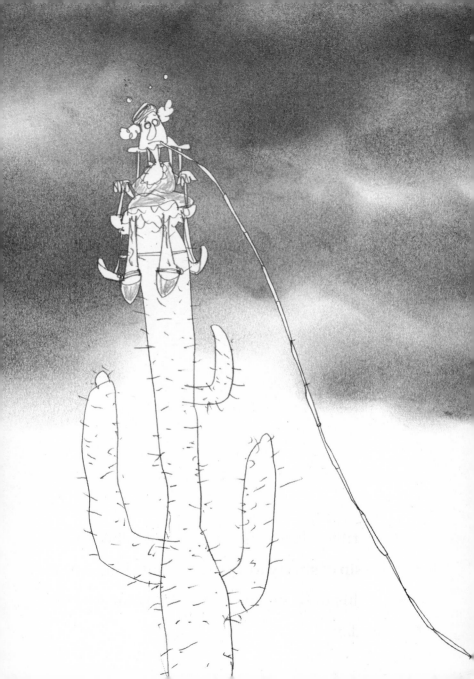

'Terrible days! Terrible days!' she cried, taking a sip of sherry from her six-mile long straw. 'Well, if this town's going down, I'm going with it! Terrible days!'

'Where ARE they?' said Friday, running past Old Granny's dangling feet. 'Those villains must be hiding SOMEWHERE!'

'Terrible days,' nodded Old Granny. 'Terrible days indeed.'

'We must of missed a bit,' said Polly, scanning the map from top to bottom. 'We must of, Mr Friday, we must!'

'No,' said Friday sadly. 'I told you – that map

shows the entire town. Every house, every street, every hill, every –'

But just then they heard a horrible noise. 'EEEEEUUUURRRRGGGH!' cried Old Granny from above.

'What is it, O.G.?' cried Polly, whipping round so fast that Alan Taylor flew out of her pocket, did a spectacular triple somersault, and landed in a palm tree.

'The – the sherry,' gasped Old Granny, gobbing out massive bits of phlegm to rid herself of the taste. 'I was just – I was just having a little sip, you know, to calm my nerves. Anyway, I was sucking on my straw and then – there was something stuck in there! So I sucked harder and – oh, it was shocking! A hoof! I swallowed a hoof!'

'What's a hoof doin' in your sherry?' said Polly. She picked up Old Granny's straw and placed the end to her lips. 'Mr Friday, is it OK if I try a little bit of sherry? I'm only nine.'

'Yes, Mr Polly,' said Friday. 'You may. It could be an important clue.' So Polly took a little sip and –

'EEEURGGGH! It tastes all meaty!' she exclaimed. 'Old Granny, where does this straw lead?'

'Why, to Finnegan's Sherry Factory on the edge of town,' said Old Granny.

'Finnegan's Sherry Factory?' said Polly. 'But that isn't on Mr Friday's map. Hang on a minute . . . O.G., do you knowed when they done opened that fact'ry?'

'Yes,' said Old Granny with a dreamy look upon her wrinkled old face. 'They opened it on the fifteenth of November, back in 1973. I shall never forget it, because it was the happiest day of my life.'

'JUMPIN' RHINOCERERS! Mr Friday, that's IT!' said Polly. 'You done drewed your map THE DAY BEFORE they opened up that fact'ry! That's why it's not on there! An' I'll bet you that's where them villains is hidin' out – an' that's why Old Granny's sherry's gone all meaty!'

'THE HOOF IS A LEMON MERINGUE! shouted Friday. 'You're right, little miss! Let's go!'

So Friday jumped on to his motorbike, which by a lucky coincidence just happened to be standing right next to him, and Polly jumped into the sidecar with Alan Taylor clinging to her hair. And they tied Old Granny's cactus-and-rocking-chair tower to the back with a rope because as she said, 'If there's sherry in trouble, I'd better come along!'

And then – **WAAAAAOOOO!**

– Friday squealed up the engine, the enormous

cactus flew out of the ground with Old Granny hanging off the end, and with a cry of 'I'VE SAID NOTHING FOR ABSOLUTELY AGES!' from Alan Taylor, they flamed it up the high street like a monstra, the rising waters lapping at their heels.

Chapter 11

Mr Gum Gets a Surprise

'It's the Ten Rules of Evil, them amazin' Rules of Evil!' sang Mr Gum and Billy as they unloaded another barrel of meat on to the furnace. 'An' you jus' will not believe all of them tricks we like to plaaaaaaaaay!'

'What a laugh it all is, Billy me old air-polluter!' grinned Mr Gum. He was covered in grease and bits of bones, and his beard was singed and blackened but none of that mattered to him now. All his thoughts were on the destruction of Lamonic Bibber, and he had never wanted anything so badly in his bad life.

'I never wanted anythin' so badly in me bad life,' roared Mr Gum as he sloshed a heap of tripe on to the flames. 'I can hardly even breathe but who even cares?'

'An' who'd've thought we was hidin' out in Finnegan's Sherry Factory what's on the edge of town miles away from anyone?' laughed Billy William the Third through a mouthful of entrails. 'No one'll ever find us here!'

'Well, that's jus' where you're wrong again!' said a voice behind them. And wheeling around, Mr Gum and Billy were confronted with the sight they hated most of all – heroes coming to save the day. Because perched on the rim of a massive vat of bubbling hot sherry were Polly, Friday, Alan Taylor, Old Granny AND a special bonus of Jake the dog, who they'd picked up along the way.

'DEPARTMENT OF CLOUDS AND YOGURTS!' chorused the heroes.

'WOOF!' chorused Jake, even though you can't really chorus on your own.

And then they did this really cool thing of

standing on each other's shoulders in an amazing human-and-dog pyramid, which was an idea Friday had come up with on the ride over.

'You're under arrests!' cried Polly from the top. 'This time you gone too far, Mr Gum, you unpleasant vine! An' I'm not very impressed with you neither, Billy William the Thirds.'

'MEDDLERS!' screamed Mr Gum. 'How the blibbin' blib did you find us, you blibbin' blibberers?'

'Cos you done carelessnesses, that's what,' said Polly, pointing to where a few hooves and entrails floated in the vat of hot, bubbling sherry.

'You MUNCHER!' roared Mr Gum, turning towards Billy. 'You been droppin' meat in the sherry an' now you've ruined everything!'

'I never,' protested Billy as he dodged a kick from Mr Gum's hobnail boot. 'I never!'

'Shabba me whiskers!' scowled Mr Gum, turning away in disgust. 'Well, come on then!'

he shouted to Polly and her friends. 'Come down here, I dares ya!'

Well, true heroes like the brave men, women, dogs and biscuits of THE DEPARTMENT OF CLOUDS AND YOGURTS do not hesitate in the face of fear. For as their motto goes:

Doo-doo-doo! Doo-doo-doo!

Doo-doo-doo!

Yeah!

And now Polly jumped down off the vat and her brave colleagues jumped down behind her, and soon the air was full of punches and smoke and heat and bacon as the final battle began.

'SNARP!' yelled Mr Gum, getting Friday in the ribs with some spare ribs.

'YISK!'

shouted Billy, as Polly
stamped on his foot.

'WOOF!'

said Jake, as he
licked up a bit of
chicken liver.

'I DO NOT CARE FOR THE WAY
YOU HAVE ABUSED THIS SHERRY
FACTORY; AND FURTHERMORE I
FIND YOUR LACK OF CONCERN

FOR THE ENVIRONMENT GREATLY DISTURBING!' exclaimed Old Granny as she swung her enormous black handbag from before the War into Mr Gum's nose.

'YAAAAA! You stupid old woman!' he cried, teetering back towards the furnace. His grotty arms pin-wheeled for balance as he regained his footing. And suddenly – FLISSSSH! – his great red beard and his stovepipe hat were aflame, and as he emerged from the furnace he uttered a yell from the very depths of his soul.

'YOU MESSED UP ME PLANS FOR THE LAST TIME!' roared Mr Gum. And now it was as if he were possessed of a strength much greater than his own, for in his fiery fury the last of any goodness that might have been inside Mr Gum was burnt up, and he was more of a monster than a man. Or a 'manster' for short.

'NAAAAAAARRGH!!' he wailed.

'FRRRRRRRRRRRRRRR-RRRRRB!'

Roaring like a chimney, Mr Gum picked up Polly and hoisted her into a corner as if she weighed but an ounce.

'SBUNVV!'

He whacked Friday across the room like a Brown Davy, the smallest species of insect known to man, which is smaller than one thousandth of an atom.

'URGO-NASURN-GRUK!'

He grimaced at Old Granny and she fell over

and everyone saw the weird old veins in her legs.

'STTTRRIIINGGG!'

He kicked Alan Taylor the entire length of the factory floor.

'NUUUURG!'

He whacked Billy in the face with a shovel.

'OW!' shouted Billy. 'Whaddya do that for?'

'Oh, yeah,' said Mr Gum, helping the poor butcher to his feet by spitting on him. 'Sorry, I gone out of me mind with uncontrollable rage there for a moment. Now come ON,' he growled.

'Let's get shovellin' again! One last barrel o'meat an' that ought to do it! One last barrel an' Lamonic Bibber slides into the sea like the idiot it is!'

The villains resumed their dark work, furiously stoking the furnace until from where she lay, limp on the floor, all Polly could see was smoke and all she could smell was meat, and all she could see was smoke. But I already told you that, pay attention.

'He . . . He . . . can'ts get away with this,'

Polly wept. Desperately she pulled herself across the factory floor. She was so tired she could hardly move – but she had to try, for she wasn't just anyone, she was Mr Polly of THE DEPARTMENT OF CLOUDS AND YOGURTS!

'Hooray,' said Polly weakly as she inched towards the villains. 'Hooray for all what's good an' lovely in the world. Hooray for snowmen. Hooray for when you wakes up an' you thinks it's school but then you remembers it's a Saturday an' there's millions of cartoons on TV. Hooray for that time I done went to that restaurant an' you was allowed to make your own desserts an' do as much ice cream as you wanted an' you could put brilliant sprinkles on top. Hooray for friends who's always stickin' up for you, even if you accident'lly break their fav'rite doll cos you was tryin' to make it fly in their back garden. Hooray for all that an' much much more! Hooray, I says, hooray!'

Mr Gum barely heard her. He was holding

a huge gristly cow heart, already aflame from the heat.

'This is it, Billy me boy!' grinned Mr Gum. 'One last bit of meat! One last bit what's gonna tip Lamonic Bibber into the sea once an' for all!'

'Yeah,' cackled Billy William, who was so excited that he'd accidentally eaten his shovel.

Mr Gum hoisted the cow heart above his head.

He brought it towards the furnace.

The sunlight blazed through the window like dragon's breath.

Billy did a burp which tasted of shovel.

'Chuck it on! Chuck it on!' he chanted.

And then –

'OH-NO-YOU-DON'TS!' cried Polly. With one last effort, she launched herself from the floor and wrestled the flaming cow heart from Mr Gum's grasp. 'You isn't never gonna beat the Forces of Good, you unbearable, unbelievable ROO-DE-LALLY!'

'Give that BACK!' yelled Mr Gum, yanking at the burning piece of meat.

'NEVER!' cried Polly, yanking back twice as hard.

The cow heart stretched as it was pulled first one way, then the other. Great orange flames spurted from its rubbery tubes.

'IT'S MINE!' yelled Mr Gum through gritted teeth.

'IT'S MINE!' yelled Polly, digging her heels in.

'IT'S MINE!' said a third voice, bursting out of nowhere. 'Yes, it is I! *Surprising Ben! I pop up here, I pop up there! Surprise! Surprise! I'm everywhere!*'

And before anyone knew what was happening, Surprising Ben grabbed the flaming cow heart for himself and off he ran, giggling like a tangerine.

'Hee hee!' he giggled. 'Hee – whoooooooooa!'

And then it was Surprising Ben's turn to get a surprise. He skidded on a scrap of tripe and the cow heart went flying from his grasp, trailing a great long streamer of fire behind it.

In the middle of the factory the vat of sherry bubbled and sloshed.

'WOOF! WOOF!'

Jake's doggy eyes tracked the cow heart as it span through the air.

'It's going to land in the sherry!' cried Old Granny. 'The factory's going to blow!'

The heroes of THE DEPARTMENT OF CLOUDS AND YOGURTS raced for the door. But Mr Gum and Billy weren't listening.

'You idiot, Billy! If you never led them meddlers here, none of this would've happened! It's all your fault!'

'MY fault? That's a laugh, Mr Gum me old gobbler!'

The flaming cow heart flew through the air . . . – 'Mr Gum! Billy! Stop your squabblin's, we gots to get out of here!'

– 'Shut up, you meddler! We're busy!'

– 'Come on, Mr Polly! Leave them to it!'

– 'I can't! I gots to save 'em, Mr Friday!'

The heart tumbled down towards the vat . . .

– 'Come *on,* Mr Polly!' shouted Friday.

– 'WOOF! WOOF!'

– 'OW! Let go of me nose, Billy me boy!'

– 'OW! No! You let go of MY nose!'

– 'No, you let go of MY –'

With a sickening splash, the flaming cow heart hit the bubbling sherry.

– 'SHABBA ME WHIS–'

plop.

Chapter 12

Clouds of Sorrow, Clouds of Joy

SHHHWWUFFF!

Friday was hurled to the ground as the factory exploded behind him. Something whizzed past his head. It was Old Granny, riding her cactus through the sky like a Mexican rocket. Alan Taylor and Jake came somersaulting along after her in a rain of broken bricks and rubble. And behind them came Surprising Ben, covered in soot and coal dust.

'Surprise! Surprise! I'm – COUGH! – *everywhere!'* he managed. And off he stumbled, wheezing like a flannel.

'Wh-what happened?' said Old Granny as she lay there on the stony ground. 'Wha–' But then she remembered, and looking back she saw one of the saddest sights of her long and drunken life. A sherry factory that would never make a single drop of sherry again.

'No,' she whispered, clutching at her heart. 'It's not fair! Why? Why? WHY?'

But Friday and Alan Taylor were scanning the wreckage with horrified expressions on their faces.

'Where is she?' breathed Alan Taylor.

'I – I don't know if she made it,' said Friday, turning his head from the flames. 'The truth is a lemon meringue,' he said softly.

And there, on the scorched grass, Friday O'Leary closed his eyes and wept hot bitter tears. And Alan Taylor staggered on to his back and hugged a couple of his vertebrae, which is as much as he was able to get his little arms around. And Old Granny forgot about the sherry and joined them and Jake lay down and whimpered softly.

And there they sat, weeping and whimpering, even as the flames grew higher and higher. Higher and higher and –

'Hiya,' said Polly. 'What you all cryin' 'bout?'

'Oh, you know,' sniffed Friday. 'Because you died in that explosion.'

'Oh,' said Polly. 'That's well sad. Mind if I joins you?'

'No, no,' said Old Granny. 'Be our guest.'

So Polly sat down on the grass and together

they all sat there crying and hugging and holding one another in their grief.

And Friday said, 'What's it like being dead, Polly?' and Polly said, 'Well, to be honest, Frides, it don't feel all that diff'rent from bein' alive really, 'cept everyone's cryin' more than usual.'

And then Alan Taylor said, 'Well, maybe you're not dead after all.'

'Well, maybe I'm not,' said Polly in astonishment.

And then everyone realised at once, and their tears of grief turned to tears of joy and their sobs turned to laughter and Jake's whimpers turned to barks of fun, and Friday turned to Polly and said, 'Look, Mr Polly. The clouds are coming back!'

And it was true, for the flames from Finnegan's Factory had reached high into the sky, licking the poisonous gases away with their soft orange tongues. And the first bits of blue were beginning to creep back overhead. And yes, the clouds were coming back, and with a sigh of relief they uncurled and began to make themselves into the fluffle-y little darlings they loved to be.

And somewhere on a high-flung branch a bluebird gave a joyful chirp and all the mosquitoes and tarantulas died because it wasn't tropical any more, but the parrots stayed alive because everyone loves parrots. And the world could breathe again.

'But hold on,' said Friday suddenly. 'What

about Mr Gum and Billy?'

Everyone turned to look at the charred remains of the factory. The villains were nowhere to be seen.

'Nothing could have survived that,' said Old Granny.

'So that's that then,' said Polly quietly. 'Mr Gum an' Billy – gone forever. They were the worst crimers what I ever saw in my life, an' they never meant no good for no one. But you knows what, Frides? It don't make me feel no happiness, it don't make me feel no happiness at all. No one deserves that, not even them two Johnny-Come-Latelys.'

Friday nodded wisely. 'Little miss, I am proud of you and your kindness towards rotters,' said he. 'But what's done is done and what's not done is not done and what's yet to be done is yet to be done and what can't be done will never be done and look at my shoelace, it's come undone.'

And as Alan Taylor said, 'We did what was right, Polly. It is the way of my people.' And as Old Granny said, 'I still can't believe the sherry factory's gone. Oh, well. Never mind.' And she took a sip of sherry from the emergency bottle she always kept hidden in Jake's fur, and it didn't taste of meat at all.

THE DEPARTMENT OF CLOUDS AND YOGURTS walked back into town and as they did so, the heavens opened and the clouds roared their approval with a torrent of lovely fresh rain to wash everyone's worries clean away. Soon the heroes were splashing and skipping merrily through the puddles like a gang of carefree bellybuttons, and Friday took out his harmonica and blew a funky little number called '**Butterscotch Betty on the Two Thirty-Nine**', and Alan Taylor rode on his hat and turned somersaults and once he fell off and Jake caught him on his tail and flipped him halfway into space for a giggle.

'Hooray for THE DEPARTMENT OF CLOUDS AND YOGURTS!' said Mayor Casserole as the heroes entered the town square. 'You've saved us all from sinking into the sea!'

'Hooray!' said the little girl called Peter. 'You've saved me and my doll!'

Then Jake ate her doll.

'Never mind,' said Peter. 'I didn't like that stupid doll anyway. She had a boy's name.'

'Hooray!' said Jonathan Ripples. 'I'm in such a good mood that I'm not even going to sit on Martin Launderette for calling me a beached whale!'

'Hooray!' said Martin Launderette.

'But *I'm* going to,' said a voice. And spinning around Martin Launderette saw a sight that made him quiver like a washing machine.

'Hello,' said the voice. 'I'm Jessica. Have you been making fun of my little brother?'

'Oh, no!' trembled Martin Launderette. 'You're even fatter than Jonath–'

But the rest of his words were lost as he was squashed under the tremendous weight of Jessica Ripples, the fattest woman in town.

And after that the lovely fresh rain stopped, and the sun came out in a blaze of triumph and a magnificent rainbow arched over the entire town, and it even had an extra stripe of 'bunch-paraka', the new colour that Friday had invented. And gazing up at that rainbow, Polly thought she heard a voice whispering, whispering to her alone.

Well done, child, the voice seemed to say, though it was no older than she. *Once again you have made the world glow with happy colours. See you around, tingler!*

And when she looked down there was a fruit chew lying at her feet, and it was a strawberry one, the best flavour of all, or at least equal with blackcurrant. And *way* better than the green ones.

'Well!' cried Mayor Casserole. 'What are we waiting for? Let's have a feast!' And soon the townsfolk were yibbing it up with the biggest and best feast of their lives. Roast ox and smoked salmon and strawberry jam, sausage rolls, Dover sole and green eggs and ham, and trifles as big as your head, my boy! Trifles as big as your head!

And Crazy Barry Fungus hopped up in his silver birdcage and everyone patted him and fed him birdseed and said what a remarkable creature he was, and they gave him the title *Birdus Magnificus* and presented him with the Order of the Golden Feather, which is the highest honour a chaffinch may be awarded.

And Old Granny announced that she was going to marry her cactus, because she had grown very fond of it, and everyone cheered and threw confetti in the air and the dancing went on all day and night, and you never did see such a thing in your life and the dish ran away with the piper's son, hickory dickory dock.

It was late in the evening, and Polly was sitting on Boaster's Hill with her friends. Jake was being Jake and Alan Taylor was being Alan Taylor, which was the way of his people. Old Granny was sipping from the bottle of sherry she always kept hidden in her cactus. And Friday – well, Friday was having a bit of a snuggle with Mrs Lovely, who had returned from an adventure of her own, battling robots in another dimension.

'You knows,' said Polly as she sat there gazing up at the soft night sky. 'Before all this, I never really thought much 'bout them clouds up there in the heavens, but now I understands how important they truly are.'

'Well said, little miss,' said Friday, strumming a lonesome chord on his blue guitar. 'You see, clouds are like people. They appear for no reason anyone can understand, they hang around for a while, and then they move on. And sometimes you don't really appreciate them until after they're gone.'

'Oh, Friday,' sighed Mrs Lovely affectionately. 'You do talk an awful lot of nonsense sometimes.'

Well, everyone nodded at that, even Friday,

and there they all sat, gazing up at the evening sky as if seeing it for the very first time. And there we shall leave them – Polly and Friday, and Mrs Lovely and Alan Taylor and Old Granny and Jake the dog and all the rest of them, gazing up at the great wide yonder and wondering at the shapes and the sights they see there. And there we shall leave them, happy in their dreams.

THE END

EPILOGUE

Portugal, one month later

*L*ittle Carlos the shepherd and his faithful sheep Splinters stumbled along the windswept hilltop.

'Come on, Splinters, you idiot,' growled Little Carlos, kicking the sheep in the rear to hurry him up. 'I gotta find a telly an' quick –

"Saco de Varas" is about to start.'

'Saco de Varas' was the Portuguese version of 'Bag of Sticks'. It was a picture of a bag of sticks for half an hour, but with Portuguese subtitles. (Little Carlos was the only person in the country who ever watched 'Saco de Varas'. Everyone else turned over to watch 'Tempo de Diversão com Crispy'.)

'Baaa! Baaaa!' said Splinters as they reached the top of the hill. Spread out below them was the friendly-looking little town of Santa del Wisp.

'Urrgh,' said Little Carlos, his big ragged beard flapping in the wind. 'What a friendly-lookin' little town. I hate it.'

But then his eyes lit up.

'Know what, Splinters, me old faithful sheep?' grinned Little Carlos. 'It looks like just the kind of place for us to get up to our evils.'

'Baaa! Baaaa! Hello,' agreed Splinters.

224

The two of them started down the hillside towards Santa del Wisp. The sun was going down and a chill was creeping into the evening air. And though they whispered it soft on the wind, if you listened carefully you could just make out the words they sang:

'Oh, you jus' will not believe all of them tricks we like to plaaaaaay . . .'

FIN

Hello again, you adorable little chestnuts. You are, aren't you? Yes, you are! You cheeky little conkers! Look at you all with your shiny little chestnut faces! Look at you all, tumbling down the hillside and rolling through the park like you haven't got a care in the world! You're simply ADORABLE! Aren't you? Aren't you? You happy little chestnuts. Yes, you are! Yes, you –

Sorry about that. I don't know what came

over me. Anyway, forget it – here's a bonus story instead. Just for you. Oh, you adorable little chestnuts. You are, aren't you? Yes, you are! You really, really are! Oh, you're just SO adora–

Sorry, everyone. Seriously, I'll shut up now. Here's the story. Sorry.

EGMONT PRESS: ETHICAL PUBLISHING

Egmont Press is about turning writers into successful authors and children into passionate readers – producing books that enrich and entertain. As a responsible children's publisher, we go even further, considering the world in which our consumers are growing up.

Safety First
Naturally, all of our books meet legal safety requirements. But we go further than this; every book with play value is tested to the highest standards – if it fails, it's back to the drawing-board.

Made Fairly
We are working to ensure that the workers involved in our supply chain – the people that make our books – are treated with fairness and respect.

Responsible Forestry
We are committed to ensuring all our papers come from environmentally and socially responsible forest sources.

For more information, please visit our website at www.egmont.co.uk/ethical

About the Author

Andy Stanton lives in North London. He studied English at Oxford but they kicked him out. He has been a film script reader, a cartoonist, an NHS lackey and lots of other things. He has many interests, but best of all he likes cartoons, books and music (even jazz). One day he'd like to live in New York or Berlin or one of those places because he's got fantasies of bohemia. His favourite expression is 'Rumble it up, Uncle Charlie!' and his favourite word is 'platypus'. This is his eighth book.

About the Illustrator

David Tazzyman lives in South London with his girlfriend, Melanie, and their son, Stanley. He grew up in Leicester, studied illustration at Manchester Metropolitan University and then travelled around Asia for three years before moving to London in 1997. He likes football, cricket, biscuits, music and drawing. He still dislikes celery.

agreeing with things much more than he liked disagreeing with things.

'Oh, look,' said Polly. 'It's a lovely bright autumn morning.'

*I*t was a lovely bright autumn morning, the sort of lovely bright autumn morning that makes you say, 'Oh, look, it's a lovely bright autumn morning.'

A Backwards Sort Of A Day

'Backwards?' suggested Friday.

'It's almost like everythin's goin'…' said Polly.

'It's true,' said Friday. 'But what is it? I can't quite put my finger on it.'

'Hold on a minute,' frowned Polly. 'Somethin's not quite right.'

Friday found disagreeing with things quite disagreeable.

'It is indeed,' agreed Friday, who liked

visit our good friend Alan Taylor up at his school on Boaster's Hill because he might have an idea what's going on and anyway it's a nice day for walking up hills and I could do with the exercise because Mrs Lovely says I'm getting a little bit portly around the belly area, which is the part of the body between your legs and your face.'

'Yeah, that's it!' exclaimed Polly as a golden-brown leaf flew up from the ground and attached itself to a tree. 'Frides, what's a-goin' on?'

what's a-goin' on?' she asked.

'That was a well long sentence what Friday just said,' thought Polly.

'Well, little miss,' said Friday, scratching his nose thoughtfully with an electronic nose-scratcher made from the leg of Hercules. 'I know all about the mysteries of time and space but I've never seen anything like this before, not in all my years, and to be honest I'm rather confused and a little bit worried, so perhaps we should go and

After a while they were quite near the top.

They weren't anywhere near the top.

It was a long walk to the top.

So off they started, up Boaster's Hill.

'Oh, I expect so,' said Friday. 'He is a headmaster after all. And headmasters know everything, like the names of famous blackcurrants and how many grains of rice there are in the sky. Come on, Polly – let's start walking.'

'Frides, do you think Alan Taylor will know

coming out to meet them. 'I'm glad you're here. What on earth's going on?'

'!PEEHC' said a bird, flying backwards through the air.

'I does hope Alan Taylor knows what's a-goin' on,' said Polly as they saw Saint Pterodactyl's School for the Poor gleaming in the sunshine on the top of the hill.

And eventually they were at the top.

Then they were very near the top.

'I said it's really rather interesting, isn't it?'

'What?' said Friday, who hadn't really been listening.

'Yes,' said Polly.

'No, absolutely no idea, I'm afraid,' said Alan Taylor, his electric muscles whirring cheerfully. 'But it's really rather interesting, isn't it?'

'Oh,' said Polly. 'We was a-hopin' you could tell us.'

'Polly! Friday!' cried little Alan Taylor,

'BARK!' said Jake and everyone laughed to
see that Polly had been right.

'I bet Jakey's gonna bark in a second,' said
Polly.

'Oh, look, here comes Jake!' cried Polly,
who loved Jake the dog more than any other dog
in the world, even that one on TV who can talk.

'Forget it,' said Alan Taylor.

'What?' said Friday. 'Sorry, I didn't hear you
that time either.'

'A old silver pocket-watch from the Victorian days what was ruled over by Queen Victorian!' she exclaimed.

Alan Taylor jumped out of Jake's mouth and handed the spit-covered object to Polly.

'What a lovely dog he is!' said Alan Taylor, climbing inside Jake's mouth and stroking his tongue affectionately. 'Hey, what's this I've found in here?'

'Oh, no!' said Polly. 'Frides, you was meant to wind it *forwards*! But you jus' gone an' wound it backwards even faster, you silly!'

So Friday took out a little key and wound up the silver pocket-watch and everyone waited to see what would happen.

'Could it somehow be controllin' Time itself?' said Polly in excitement.

'And look,' said Friday. 'It's running backwards! The hands are moving the wrong way!'

THE END

'We'll fix it in a minute,' laughed Alan Taylor as a nearby sparrow turned into a dinosaur. 'But not just yet – this is the coolest thing I've ever seen in my life!'

'Oops,' said Friday as they sat there watching the trees turning into seeds, the passers-by turning into ancient Romans and the sun setting and rising over and over again.